The Little
Dutch Boy
A Tale of Perseverance

Louis Weber, C.E.O.
Publications International, Ltd.
7373 North Cicero Avenue
Lincolnwood, Illinois 60646.

Manufactured in China.

8 7 6 5 4 3 2 1

ISBN 0-7853-2921-8

The Little Dutch Boy
A Tale of Perseverance

Illustrated by Linda Dockey Graves

Adapted by Sarah Toast

Publications International, Ltd.

Long ago there was a boy named Hans who lived with his mother in a pretty town in Holland. The land of Holland is very flat, and much of it is below the level of the sea. The farmers there built big walls called dikes to keep the sea from flooding their farms. Hans and the other children knew that if a dike broke, the fields and towns would be ruined.

One day Hans's mother packed a basket of fruit, bread, and cheese for Hans to take to their old friend, Mr. Van Notten. Mr. Van Notten lived outside of town, and it was a long way to his house. Even though Hans was just a little boy, he could walk there by himself. His mother had shown him the way.

As Hans set out, his mother told him not to stay too late. She wanted him to be home before dark.

Mr. Van Notten had only an old dog to keep him company, so he was very happy when Hans came to visit him. To get to Mr. Van Notten's home, Hans just followed the main road out of town. The road ran right alongside the dike.

Hans was very thirsty and hungry after his long walk, so Mr. Van Notten made cocoa and set out the bread and cheese. After their meal, they talked by the fire. Hans enjoyed Mr. Van Notten's stories about life in Holland when the old man was a little boy.

When Mr. Van Notten's dog scratched at the door to be let out, Hans noticed that the sky had become dark and stormy. He decided that he should leave right away to get home before it started to rain. Hans said good-bye to Mr. Van Notten and promised to come back soon.

Hans walked quickly, but he was not even halfway home when the air became much colder and the wind began to blow very hard. It wasn't long before cold, stinging raindrops battered Hans as he struggled against the powerful wind. The weather made it difficult for Hans to walk, but he kept going. "If I just keep putting one foot in front of the other," said Hans to himself, "I'll be home soon."

The strong wind made the trees bend low, and it flattened the flowers. Hans had to hold his hat to keep it from blowing away. "I hope my mother isn't upset when she sees me so cold and wet," he thought.

Hans was getting more and more tired with every step, but he had to keep going. He remembered that his mother wanted him home before dark. Hans wanted to get home so she would not worry.

Hans kept his head down against the strong wind as he trudged along the road. It was so dark outside that Hans had no idea he was close to town until he lifted his head for a moment. Hans was happy to see the dike right in front of him. It meant he would soon be home and out of the cold rain.

Even with all the raindrops falling and dripping from the trees, Hans noticed some water where it shouldn't have been. There was a small hole in the dike, and a trickle of water was seeping through.

Hans knew right away what must have happened. The storm had whipped up the waves of the sea on the other side, and the great weight of the pounding water made a crack in the dike.

"I've got to warn everybody that the dike has sprung a leak!" thought Hans.

"The dike is breaking!" Hans shouted, as he ran into town. "Help! We've got to fix the dike!"

Shout as he would, no one heard Hans. Nobody else was outside, and all the houses had been completely shut. All the doors were secured tightly and bolted, every window closed and shuttered.

Hans soon realized his shouting wasn't doing any good. He stopped running to catch his breath. Leaning against a fence, Hans tried to think of a plan.

Hans knew his mother must be worrying about him, but he also knew that the tiny hole in the dike was getting bigger every minute. If the hole got big enough, the sea would surely push its way through and break the dike. If the dike broke, the sea would flood the farms and wash away the pretty little town.

As fast as he could, Hans ran back to the place where he had seen the crack in the dike. Sure enough, the crack was quickly growing wider. Hans knew that it must be fixed soon. Otherwise the sea would break through, and it would be too late. There was nothing else to do, so Hans balled up his fist and pushed it into the hole to stop the little stream of water.

Hans was proud and happy that one small boy could hold back the sea. He was sure that his mother would soon send people to look for him. But minutes became hours as Hans patiently waited.

As darkness fell Hans became very cold and tired. His arm began to ache. He had to force himself to keep standing on his tired legs. To keep himself going, Hans thought about how important it was to hold back the water of the sea.

As Hans stood in the rain by the dike, he thought about his home and its warm fireplace. Then he thought about how good it was going to feel to lie down in his snug bed. These thoughts helped the exhausted boy get through the long and cold night.

When Hans didn't come home that evening, his mother began to worry. Even while the rain was falling, she kept looking out the door for Hans to come back. At last she decided that Hans must have waited out the storm at Mr. Van Notten's. She thought he must have spent the night there because it was too dark to come home after the storm.

After looking out the door one more time, Hans's mother closed up the house and went to bed, but she couldn't sleep. She was too worried about her little boy.

Early the next morning, Mr. Van Notten was walking to Hans's home. He wanted to thank Hans for the visit and thank his mother for the tasty food. When he came to where Hans was, the boy was trembling with cold. Hans's arm hurt from keeping his fist in the hole of the dike. His legs were ready to collapse from standing all night. Still Hans had to hold firm for just a little while longer so Mr. Van Notten could run to get help. "Don't worry, Hans," said Mr. Van Notten. "I'll be back in a jiffy. Just hang on a little longer."

Soon Mr. Van Notten returned with someone to take care of Hans. He also brought materials to repair the dike.

Hans was wrapped in blankets and taken home. He was put to bed and given warm broth to drink. His mother rubbed his stiff legs and fingers.

Word quickly spread through the town of how Hans had held back the sea. The townspeople were very curious. They went to the dike to see the hole that Hans had bravely kept plugged.

As soon as Hans felt strong enough, he and his mother went back to the dike to see the repairs that were being made. Everyone in town was overjoyed to see Hans. They thanked the little boy for holding back the sea and for saving them from what would otherwise have been a terrible flood.

The mayor of the town presented Hans with a medal to honor his dedication, and all the townspeople cheered loudly. Hans would forever after be remembered as a hero. Years later, even after Hans was all grown up, people still called him the little boy with the big heart.

One to Grow On
Perseverance

When Hans discovered a leak in the dike that held back the sea, he knew it had to be stopped. Because he couldn't find help, he plugged up the leak himself and stood his ground for hours and hours. Even though it was dark and cold in the storm, Hans knew that he was the only person who could keep the town from being washed away. That kind of dedication is called perseverance.

Perseverance means not giving up even when something gets difficult. It helps us get through hard times so that we can accomplish great things.

The End